Bumper
Funny Joke

More than 1000 side-splitting jokes to make you laugh out loud

Suitable for ages 5-8, 9-12, 13-99 and beyond.

Robbie Johnson

Illustrated by

John Martin

Published by

LIFERAFTMEDIA Ltd

LIFERAFTMEDIA Ltd

www.liferaftmedia.com

First published 2020

Print ISBN: 978-1-913514-02-0
Kindle ISBN: 978-1-913514-03-7
eBook/Other ISBN: 978-1-913514-04-4

Contents

Knock-knock Jokes

Knock knock.
Who's there?
The Queen.
The Queen who?
The Queen-er to Quean your house!

Knock knock.
Who's there?
Eileen.
Eileen who?
Eileen-d over to ring the bell but I can't reach!

Knock knock.
Who's there?
Jamaican.
Jamaican who?
Jamaican me crazy, just let me in!

Knock Knock.
Who's there?
Avenue.
Avenue who?
Avenue kept me waiting long enough?

Knock knock.
Who's there?
Annie.
Annie who?
Annie-body there?

Knock knock.
Who's there?
Theodore.
Theodore who?
Theodore won't open!

DID YOU KNOW...?
Kangaroos cannot walk backwards.

Knock Knock.
Who's there?
Honey bee.
Honey bee who?
Honey bee a dear and open the door please.

Knock knock.
Who's there?
Ira.
Ira who?
Ira-gret to inform you that I really need to come in.

Knock knock.
Who's there?
Doris.
Doris who?
Doris still locked, please let me in!

Knock Knock.
Who's there?
Jess.
Jess who?
Jess let me in, I'm fed up of asking!

Knock knock.
Who's there?
Scott.
Scott who?
Scott to be time
to let me in!

Knock knock.
Who's there?
Nun.
Nun who?
Nun of your business just let me in!

Knock Knock.
Who's there?
Cindy.
Cindy who?
Cindy (It's in the) invitation.
You're supposed to let me in!

TIME FOR A TONGUE TWISTER...

Any noise annoys an oyster but a noisy noise annoys an oyster more.

Knock knock.
Who's there?
Shirley.
Shirley who?
Shirley you can see the door is locked. Let me in!

Knock Knock.
Who's there?
Matt.
Matt who?
Matt my wit's end now – open the door!

Knock knock.
Who's there?
Dewey.
Dewey who?
Dewey really have to keep going on like this? Just let me in!

Knock knock.
Who's there?
Gnome.
Gnome who?
Gnome matter how long you keep me waiting, I'll keep knocking!

Knock knock.
Who's there?
Bed.
Bed who?
Bed-tween me and you,
I think your doorbell is broken.

Knock knock.
Who's there?
Gus.
Gus who?
Gus I'd better just keep knocking.

Knock knock.
Who's there?
Imogen.
Imogen who?
Imogen how nice it would be if you'd let me in.

Knock knock.
Who's there?
Felix.
Felix who?
Felix-cited about letting me in yet?

Knock knock.
Who's there?
Spain.
Spain who?
Spain in the neck having to wait out here – let me in!

KNOCK KNOCK.
Who's there?
Kim.
Kim who?
Kim ON, JuST Let Me IN!

Knock knock.
Who's there?
Eve.
Eve who?
Eve-n though you're smelly, I still want to come in!

DID YOU KNOW...?
Hippopotamus milk is pink.

Knock knock.
Who's there?
Jen.
Jen who?
Jen-erally, people open the door when someone knocks!

Knock knock.
Who's there?
Don.
Don who?
Don ask questions, just open the door!

Knock Knock.
Who's there?
Cereal.
Cereal who?
Cereal shame I have to wait like this.

Knock Knock.
Who's there?
Stopwatch.
Stopwatch who?
Stopwatch you are doing and let me in!

Knock Knock.
Who's there?
Police.
Police who?
Police let me in!

Knock knock.
Who's there?
Icy.
Icy who?
Icy you in there, open up!

Knock knock.
Who's there?
Pasta.
Pasta who?
Pasta key out,
I'll open the door myself!

Knock knock.
Who's there?
Iris.
Iris who?
Iris-ked a lot to come here,
so please let me in!

Knock knock.
Who's there?
Atlas.
Atlas who?
Atlas-t! Open the door!

TIME FOR A TONGUE TWISTER...

Many mumbling mice are making merry music in the moonlight.

Knock knock.
Who's there?
Alma.
Alma who?
Alma friends are already here – can I come too?

Knock knock.
Who's there?
Howl.
Howl who?
Howl you know unless you open up?

Knock knock.
Who's there?
Snow.
Snow who?
Snow way I'm staying out here all night!

Knock knock.
Who's there?
Pudding.
Pudding who?
Pudding a doorbell out here would be helpful!

Knock knock.
Who's there?
Hugh.
Hugh who?
You don't need to repeat yourself – just open the door

DID YOU KNOW...?
It is impossible for most people to lick their own elbow.

Knock Knock.
Who's there?
Lou.
Lou who?
No not loo who. I need the LOO! PLEASE let me in!

Knock Knock.
Who's there?
Alex.
Alex who?
Alexplain if you let me in!

Knock knock.
Who's there?
Albie.
Albie who?
Albie knocking all night if you don't let me in!

Knock knock.
Who's there?
Snot.
Snot who?
Snot fair keeping me waiting like this!

Knock knock.
Who's there?
Alan.
Alan who?
Alan-vite you to my party if you let me in.

Knock knock.
Who's there?
Eva.
Eva who?
Eva had someone knock on your door this many times?

Knock knock.
Who's there?
Neil.
Neil who?
Neil down and look through the letterbox!

Knock knock.
Who's there?
Wooden.
Wooden who?
Wooden it be nice to open the door?

Knock knock.
Who's there?
Liner.
Liner who?
Liner-round all day isn't good for you – open the door.

Knock knock.
Who's there?
Ali.
Ali who?
Ali-v you alone if you open the door

Knock knock.
Who's there?
Bro.
Bro who?
Bro-ke your bell, sorry.
That's why I'm knocking!

Knock knock.
Who's there?
Arthur.
Arthur who?
Arthur any other doors
I can knock on?

Knock knock.
Who's there?
Acid.
Acid who?
Acid my name already, open up!

TIME FOR A TONGUE TWISTER...

**If a woodchuck could chuck wood,
how much wood would a woodchuck chuck,
if a woodchuck could chuck wood?**

Knock Knock.
Who's there?
A fish.
A fish who?
A fish-ially annoyed now – open the door!

Knock knock.
Who's there?
Gino.
Gino who?
**Gino what?
I'll just go somewhere else!**

Knock knock.
Who's there?
Justin.
Justin who?
Justin time, I was about to leave!

Knock Knock.
Who's there?
Owls.
Owls who?
Yes, you're right, they do!

Knock Knock.
Who's there?
Dogs say.
Dogs say who?
No, dogs say "woof."

Knock Knock.
Who's there?
Cows go.
Cows go who?
No, cows go "moo!"

Knock Knock.
Who's there?
Cargo.
Cargo who?
No, cargo vroooooom!

Knock Knock.
Who's there?
Who.
Who who?
Are you an owl too?

Knock Knock.
Who's there?
Turnip.
Turnip who?
Turnip the volume,
I can't hear you!

DID YOU KNOW...?
11% of people are left handed.

Knock Knock.
Who's there?
Cook.
Cook who?
You're a cuckoo now?

Knock knock.
Who's there?
Little old lady.
Little old lady who?
Wow, I didn't know you could yodel.

Knock Knock.
Who's there?
Spell.
Spell who?
W-H-O.

Knock knock
Who's there?
Say.
Say who?
Who!

Knock Knock.
Who's there?
Woo.
Woo who?
What are you so excited about?

Knock knock.
Who's there?
Oswald.
Oswald who?
Oswald my chewing gum by accident!

Knock Knock.
Who's there?
Kenya.
Kenya who?
Kenya not tell by my voice?

Knock Knock.
Who's there?
Milo.
Milo who?
Milo-d of laundry is almost done can I come in now?

Knock knock.
Who's there?
Europe.
Europe who?
Europe early today!

Knock Knock.
Who's there?
Emma.
Emma who?
Emma little bit late, I'm sorry!

Knock knock.
Who's there?
Candice.
Candice who?
Candice door open any faster?

TIME FOR A TONGUE TWISTER...

Fuzzy Wuzzy was a bear,
Fuzzy Wuzzy had no hair,
Fuzzy Wuzzy wasn't very fuzzy, was he?

Knock Knock.
Who's there?
Heidi.
Heidi who?
Heidi key under the door mat next time so I don't have to knock

Knock knock.
Who's there?
Comb.
Comb who?
Comb and open the door!

Knock knock.

Who's there?

Noah.

Noah who?

Noah good place to get a burger?

Knock knock.

Who's there?

Alaska.

Alaska who?

**Alaska-nother house,
maybe they'll let me in!**

Knock knock.
Who's there?
Ida.
Ida who?
Ida-like to come in please!

Knock knock.
Who's there?
Fred.
Fred who?
Fred I can't tell you until you let me in!

Knock knock.
Who's there?
I'm Gladys.
I'm Gladys who?
I'm Gladys almost my birthday!

Knock knock.
Who's there?
Passion.
Passion who?
Passion by your house, so I thought I'd stop by!

DID YOU KNOW...?
The chameleon has a tongue that is 1.5 times the length of its body.

Knock knock.
Who's there?
Joy.
Joy who?
Joy-n me for a walk?

Knock knock.
Who's there?
Tennis.
Tennis who?
Tenn-is too late –
I want to come in now!

Knock knock.
Who's there?
Theresa.
Theresa who?
Theresa beautiful
this time of year aren't they?

Knock knock.
Who's there?
Closure.
Closure who?
Closure windows, it's raining!

Knock knock.

Who's there?

Carrie.

Carrie who?

Carrie these bags in for me please!

TIME FOR A TONGUE TWISTER...

She sells sea shells by the seashore, and the shells that she sells are sea shells for sure.

Knock knock.
Who's there?
Matthew.
Matthew who?
Matthew lace needs to be tied can you help me?

Knock knock.
Who's there?
Leaf.
Leaf who.
Leaf me alone!

Knock knock.
Who's there?
Handsome.
Handsome who?
Handsome keys out and I'll open the door myself!

DID YOU KNOW...?
Sea otters hold hands when they sleep to keep from drifting apart.

Knock knock.
Who's there?
Esme.
Esme who?
Esme lunch ready yet?

Knock knock.
Who's there?
Phillip.
Phillip who?
Phillip the car with petrol and let's go!

Knock knock.
Who's there?
Hugo.
Hugo who?
Hugo this way, I'll go that way.

Knock knock.
Who's there?
Walter.
Walter who?
Walter wall carpet.

Knock knock.
Who's there?
Joanna.
Joanna who?
Joanna come out to play?

Knock knock.
Who's there?
Soup.
Soup who?
Soup-er Man

Knock knock.
Who's there?
Fiona.
Fiona who?
Fiona me a taxi I want to go home.

Knock knock.
Who's there?
Joan.
Joan who?
Joan a lawnmower
I can borrow please?

Knock knock.
Who's there?
Watcher.
Watcher who?
Watcher name?
I'm doing a survey.

Knock knock.
Who's there?
Papa.
Papa who?
Papa ya head round the door and you'll see!

Knock knock.
Who's there?
Ammonia.
Ammonia who?
Ammonia small person, please let me in!

Knock knock.
Who's there?
Michael.
Michael who?
Michael-lection of toys is very big would you like to see it?

Knock knock.
Who's there?
Picture.
Picture who?
Picture coat on and come out to play!

Knock knock.
Who's there?
Alf.
Alf who?
Alf-orget why I'm here
if you don't open up soon!

Knock knock.
Who's there?
Isla.
Isla who?
Isla-v you so much!

Knock knock.
Who's there?
A nap.
A nap who?
A nap-ple a day
keeps the doctor away!

Knock knock.
Who's there?
A guest.
A guest who?
A guest you'd ask that, it's me!

Knock knock.
Who's there?
Edith.
Edith who?
Edith game is going on and on!

Knock knock.
Who's there?
Honeydew.
Honeydew who?
Honeydew know how much I love you?

Knock knock.
Who's there?
Jenny.
Jenny who?
Jenny-d a hand to open the door?

Knock knock.
Who's there?
Ron.
Ron who?
Ron house, I'm sorry!

Knock knock.
Who's there?
Diploma.
Diploma who?
Diploma to fix your toilet.

DID YOU KNOW...?

Monkeys can go bald in old age, just like humans.

Knock knock.

Who's there?

Fur.

Fur who?

Furget it, I'll just go home.

Q and A Jokes

Food/Drink

What would you call fake spaghetti?

An im*pasta*.

What did the salads say when they were locked out of the fridge?

"*Lettuce* in!"

Why did the girl put a cake in the freezer?

She wanted to ice it!

What do penguins put in their salads?

Iceberg lettuce.

What continent is like bacon?

Europe, because it has Greece.

When is it okay to go at red and stop at green?

When you're eating watermelon!

What is the proof that carrots are good for your eyes?

You've never seen a rabbit wearing glasses, have you?

DID YOU KNOW...?
Turtles can breathe through their bottoms.

How can you tell where the Easter Bunny hides his treasure?

Eggs marks the spot.

What do rabbits wear when they get engaged?

14 *carrot* diamond rings.

What do zombies put on their Sunday dinner?

Grave-y.

How do monsters prefer their eggs cooked?

Terri-fried.

Why do snowmen love cake?

Because they love icing.

What is the best type of key to eat?

A tur*key*.

What berry is the saddest?

A *blue*berry.

What letter makes the best drink?

T.

Why was the pizza so rich?

Because it had a lot of dough!

What did the boy grape say to the girl grape?

I've got a *crush* on you.

What is a math teacher's favourite food?

Pie.

Why did the celery lock its doors and close the curtains?

Because it was afraid it was being stalked!

What did the butter say when it did a good job?

"I'm on a roll!"

Why did the policeman put a piece of toast on the road?

Because there was a traffic *jam*.

What is a cat's favourite breakfast cereal?

Mice Krispies

What do you get if you put hot water down a rabbit hole?

Hot cross bunnies.

TIME FOR A TONGUE TWISTER...

Betty Botter bought a bit of butter but the bit of butter was too bitter, so Betty bought a better bit of butter to make the bitter butter better.

What do birds eat for breakfast?

*Flap*jacks.

What is a cow's favourite drink?

A s*moo*thie.

Why did the orange go to the hospital?

Because it wasn't peeling very well!

What is a penguin's favourite food to eat at a BBQ?

*Ice*bergers.

What do ducks eat for a snack?

Cheese and *quack*ers.

What do pigs do when they go to the park?

They have a *pig*nic.

How do ducks break eggs?

They quack them!

What do you get when you cross a cow with a trampoline?

A milk*shake*.

What kind of fizzy drink do dolphins like?
Ginger *whale.*

What is yellow and dangerous?
A banana with a machine gun.

Why did the apple stop running?
It ran out of juice!

What is a snowman's favourite food?
Chilli.

What's yellow and sniffs?
A banana with a cold.

What's the fastest vegetable?
A runner bean.

What is a chip's favourite day of the week?
*Fry*day.

What do ghosts eat with meatballs?
*Spook*hetti.

How do you fix fruit?

You re*pear* it!

What does an egg say when it messes around?

"I'm only *yolk*ing."

What did the fast tomato say to the slower tomato?

"Try to ketchup!"

What is a monster's favourite dessert?

Ice *scream*.

What pudding is brown and has antlers?

Chocolate *moose*.

What do you call pasta that you spill on your leg?

Macaro*knee*.

What fruit do vampires love to eat?

*Neck*tarines.

DID YOU KNOW...?

Taumatawhakatangihangako auauotamateaturipukakapikimau Hill in New Zealand is the world's longest place name.

Why did the honeydew melon jump in the lake?

Because it wanted to be a *water*melon.

Where do you learn to make ice cream?

At *sundae* school.

What kind of corn can't you eat?

A *uni*corn.

What's yummy and goes to space?

A rocket *chip*.

What fruit is the best to sit on?

*Chair*ries.

What do monsters put on their sandwiches?

*Scream*cheese.

Where does spaghetti go to dance?

To the meatball.

What is a scarecrow's favourite food?

*Straw*berries.

What is a monster's favourite ice cream flavour?

Cookies and *scream*.

What's a cat's favourite food?

Mice cream.

Why don't eggs tell jokes?

They'd crack up.

What kind of room has no doors?

A mushroom.

Why does the mushroom always get invited to parties?

Because he's a fungi (fun guy).

Did you hear the rumour about butter?
I'm not going to tell you – you'll spread it.

Do you want to hear a joke about pizza?
Never mind, it's very cheesy.

Why did the onion call for help?
He was in a pickle.

Why shouldn't you make fun of an egg?
They can't take a yolk.

What's the difference between an elephant and a biscuit?
You can't dip an elephant in your tea.

What is long, green and perfectly still?
A cucumber holding its breath.

Why did the orange go out with the prune?
Because he couldn't find a date.

What do you get when you put four ducks in a box?

A box of quackers.

What did the mayonnaise say to the fridge?

Close the door, I'm dressing.

Why did the tomato blush?

Because he saw the salad dressing.

Did you hear about the Italian chef that died?

He pasta way.

What does a grape say when it gets stepped on?

Nothing, it just lets out a little wine.

How do make a hot dog stand?

Take away his chair.

I always confuse chutney and pickle.

It makes me chuckle.

What's white, fluffy and hangs around in cake shops?

A meringue-utang.

What is a frog's favourite flavour of crisp?

Croaky bacon.

How can you tell if there was elephant in your fridge?

There are footprints in the butter.

What is two words long and has dozens of letters?

Alphabet soup.

How do you make an egg roll?

Place it at the top of a hill and let it go.

Creatures

Why do fish avoid computers?

So they don't get caught in the internet.

What do gorillas learn at school?

Their Ape, B C's.

What's white on the outside, green on the inside and comes with ketchup & onions?

A hot frog.

What do you get if you cross a sheep and a porcupine?

An animal that knits its own jumpers.

What do you get if cross a kangaroo and a sheep?

A woolly jumper.

What flies around the school room late at night?

The alpha BAT.

Why do hummingbirds hum?

They can't remember the words.

How do spiders communicate?

On the World Wide Web.

What do you call a crocodile wearing a vest?

An investigator!

TIME FOR A TONGUE TWISTER...
Six slimy snails slid slowly seaward.

How do Indian Elephants communicate with African elephants?

They use an elephone.

What do you call a tiger at the North Pole?

Lost.

What happens when cows refuse to be milked?

Udder chaos.

What do you get when you cross a chicken and a centipede?

Enough drumsticks for everyone.

How does a penguin build its house?

Igloos it together.

What happened to the frog's car when it broke down?

It got toad away.

What do you call a camel with no hump?

Humphrey.

Where does a rabbit go after its wedding?

On a *bunny*moon.

How do cows do maths?

With a cowculator.

What's the difference between a fish and a guitar?

You can tune a guitar, but you can't tuna fish.

What did the fish say when it swam into the wall?

Dam.

What happens when giraffes try to drive cars?

They end up in a giraffic jam.

What do you get when you cross a millipede with a parrot?

A walkie talkie.

DID YOU KNOW...?
Octopuses have three hearts.

How did the little dog feel when it saw the big scary dog?

Terrier-fied.

What is it called when a cat wins a dog show?

A cat-has-trophy.

What do you call an elephant that doesn't matter?

Irrelephant.

What time was it when the elephant sat on the fence?

Time to get a new fence.

What is black and white and red all over?

A penguin with sunburn.

What do giraffes have such long necks?
Because their feet smell so bad.

Why are elephants so wrinkly?
They don't fit on the ironing board.

Where do sheep go on holiday?
The *Baaa* hamas.

Why couldn't the pony sing to her friends?

Because he was a little hoarse.

What is a frog's favourite drink?

Croak a cola.

What did the teacher say to the horse as he entered the classroom?

Why the long face?

Why can't you play cards in the jungle?

It's full of Cheetahs.

Why are cats so good at singing?

Because they're so *mew*sical.

What do you sing to a sheep on its birthday?

Happy birthday to *ewe*."

DID YOU KNOW...?

Bees can fly higher than Mount Everest.

What did the waiter at the restaurant say to the dog?

Bone-appetit!

What is the smartest animal in the ocean?

Fish, because they go to school.

How do bears keep their caves cool?

With *bear* conditioning.

What do you call a dog that does magic tricks?

A labracadabrador!

What holiday do cows love celebrating the most?

Moo Years Day.

Why do frogs always lie?

Because they're am-*fib*-ians.

Why do dolphins swim in saltwater?

Because pepper water makes them sneeze!

Where do cow students eat?

In the *calf*eteria.

How do you know if an elephant is hiding under your couch?

You keep banging your head on the ceiling!

What bird needs to wear a wig?

A bald eagle!

How do you stop a rhinoceros from charging?

Unplug it.

What do you call a fly that lost its wings?

A walk!

What do pigs use when they have a rash?

*Oink*ment.

What kind of keys cannot open doors?

Monkeys and donkeys.

What do you call a chicken with three eyes?
A chiiicken.

What is a rabbit's favourite kind of music?
Hip hop.

How do bees make their hair look nice?
They use a honeycomb!

How does an octopus make you laugh?
With ten *tickles*.

What do you call it when a cow gets in a car accident?
An udder tragedy.

What did the cow do when she was scared?
Turned and ran the *udder* direction.

What is a shark's favourite country?
*Fin*land.

What do you get when you cross a pig with a dinosaur?

Jurassic *Pork*.

What did the dolphin say when he crashed into a boat?

Sorry, I didn't do it on *porpoise*.

What is a polar bear's favourite food?

A *brrr-grrr.*

Which are the strongest animals in the ocean?

Mussels.

Where do pet birds go on holiday?

To the *Canary* Islands.

What happened when the two rabbits fell in love?

They lived hoppily ever after.

How does an oyster get to the hospital?

A clambulance.

Why do chickens lay their eggs?

Because if they dropped them they would break.

DID YOU KNOW...?

A crocodile cannot stick its tongue out.

How does a dog like his eggs cooked?
Pooched.

Why do geese fly south during the winter?
Because it would be too far to walk.

Why do hummingbirds hum?
Because they don't know the words to the song!

What do you call a chicken that wakes you up?
An alarm *cluck*.

What is a bird's favourite type of math?
*Owl*gebra.

What do you call a phony polar bear?
A snow*fake*.

What is a pig's favourite type of wood?
Ma*hog*any.

Why did the bird carry the clock?

To see time fly!

What did the octopus say after telling a joke?

"Just *squid*ing."

What do you call it when an insect and a dear run away to get married?

Ant-elope.

Can one exotic bird be a pair?

No, but *toucan*.

What do you call a monkey with a bomb?

A ba*boom*.

What do you call it when a horse tells a story?

A pony *tale*.

What looks like half a donkey?

The other half.

TIME FOR A TONGUE TWISTER...
A big black bug bit a big black dog on his big black nose.

What's it called when you mistake a terrapin for a tortoise?

A turtle disaster.

What do you get if you cross an insect with the Easter rabbit?

Bugs bunny.

Why are leopards the worst animal at hide-and-seek?

Because they're always spotted.

What do you call a deer with no eyes?

No idea.

What do you call a deer with no eyes and no legs?

Still no idea.

What do you call a deer with no ear?

D

What's black and white, black and white, black and white?

A penguin rolling down a hill.

What do you call a gorilla with a banana in each ear?

Anything you like, he can't hear you.

What do you call a crocodile that steals things?

A crook-odile.

How do bees get to school?

By school buzz.

How do fish get to school?

By octobus.

DID YOU KNOW...?

Octopuses lay 56,000 eggs at a time.

What do you call a bull that's asleep?

A bull-dozer.

Where do fish keep their money?

At the riverbank.

Where do you find out how heavy a whale is?

Take it to the Whale Weigh Station.

What do you call a sheep on a trampoline?

A woolly jumper.

Where do you find a dog with no legs?

Where you left it.

Why did the chicken cross the playground?

To get to the other slide.

Why did the lion cross the road?

To get to the other pride.

What do you call a dog who can tell time?

A watchdog!

Why did the piece of chewing gum cross the road?

Because it was stuck to the bottom of the chicken's foot!

Why did the fox cross the road?

It wanted to get the chicken.

Why did the dog cross the road?

It was the chicken's day off.

Why did the chicken cross the road again and again and again?

It was chasing a boomerang.

Why did the duck cross the road?

Because it thought it was a chicken.

Why did the chicken stop crossing the road?

He was fed up with all the chicken jokes.

What goes 99-clonk, 99-clonk, 99-clonk?

A centipede with a wooden leg.

What do snakes learn at school?

Hiss.....tory.

Why do cows wear bells?

Because their horns don't work.

Why did the dog sit in front of the fire?

Because he wanted to be a hot dog.

What should a dog do when it meets the queen?

Bow wow.

How do dogs talk to trees?

They bark!

What do cats say when they get hurt?

"Me*OW*!"

Where did the cat keep her money?

In her *purr*se.

How does a frog watch movies?

On a lil-iPad.

What time do ducks get up?

At the quack of dawn.

What did the turtle do on its birthday?

It had a *shell*ebration.

How did the frog feel when its toy broke?

Un*hoppy*.

Why did the chicken get the duck a cake?

Because it was its *bird*day.

Where do sheep take a bath?

In the *baaaa*thtub.

How do farmers do maths?

They use a *cow*culator!

What do you call a dancing sheep?

A *baa*lerina.

What do you call a dog who goes to school?

Teacher's pet.

Why did the rabbit go to the hospital?

It needed a *hop*eration.

Why did the crab not want to share?

Because it was shellfish!

What do you call it when a duck causes the ground to shake?

An earth*quack*.

DID YOU KNOW...?
A giraffe has just seven bones in its neck - the same as a human!

How do you start a teddy bears' race?

You say "teddy, set, go!"

Why did the cat chase the computer?

Because it had a mouse!

What do you call a pile of kittens?

A *meow*ntain.

What did the frog teacher tell his student to do to the paper?

"Rip-it."

Can a puppy open a door?

No, it's im*paw*sible.

What do fish sleep in?

Water beds.

What do little dogs use to wash their hair?

Sham*poodle*.

What do you call a rabbit with fleas?

Bugs Bunny.

What does the Easter Bunny do in the gym?

Eggs-ercizes.

What do you call a donkey with 3 legs?

A wonkey.

What do you call a very cold dog?

A pupsicle.

What's a dog's favourite pizza topping?

*Pup*peroni.

What would you call a bear that doesn't have teeth?

A gummy bear!

What kind of bug can be found on a clock?

A tick.

What do you call a clever reindeer?

*A brain*deer.

Why are cats the best pets?

Because they are just *purr*fect.

What does a dog press when it wants a movie to stop?

The *paws* button.

What animal on the farm is the quietest?

A *shhh*eep.

What do whales take to stay healthy?

Vitamin Sea.

Where do sheep go to get haircuts?

At the *baa-baas.*

Where do penguins go to dance?

To *snow*balls.

What's a fish's favourite game?

Salmon says.

What do you call a crab wearing a red coat, red hat and black boots?

Sandy claws.

What did the snake give his girlfriend?

A hug and a hiss.

What is a mouse's favourite game?

Hide and *squeak*.

What do you call for a pig when it gets hurt?

The *ham*bulance.

What do little pigs do when they get home from school?

Their *ham*work.

Who is the insect's uncle married to?

His ant.

What dog helps you get in buildings?

A labra*door*.

What do you call a puppy stuck outside in the rain?

A soggy doggy!

What time do ducks get up?

At the quack of dawn.

Which side of a chicken has the most feathers?

The outside.

What's it called when a cat has a nasty accident?

A *cat*astrophe.

What does an elephant wear to the beach?

Swimming trunks.

DID YOU KNOW...?
Fleas can jump a height of up to 60 times their own body length.

What do birds say on Halloween?
"Trick or *tweet*!"

What fish are the best at fighting?
*Sword*fish.

General

Why was the maths teacher so upset?
Because she had too many problems!

Why did the vampire study?
Because it had a blood test.

What do you call an annoying scarf?
A pain in the neck!

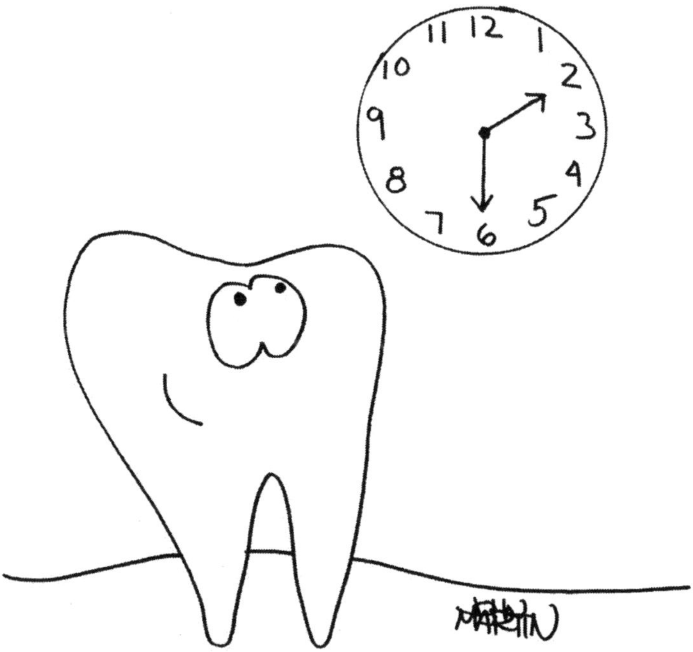

When is the best time to go to the dentist?

At tooth-hurty.

What do you call someone with a nose but no body?

Nobody knows.

What kind of candy do prisoners hate?

Candy *bars*.

Why are Saturday and Sunday so strong?

Because they aren't *weak*days.

How did the electrician feel when he got his wires mixed up?

Shocked!

What did the calculator say to the child in maths class?

"You can count on me!"

What sort of music do doctors like?

Anything with a good heart*beat*.

What do you call a snowman's money?

Cold hard cash!

How could you tell that the cemetery was popular?

Because people were *dying* to get in.

Why did the vampire get a pencil and paper?

Because he wanted to draw blood.

What did one wall say to the other wall?

I'll meet you at the corner.

What do monsters put in their hair?

*Scare*spray.

What do librarians like to do in the garden?

Weed books.

What kind of button doesn't go on clothes?

A belly button.

What did the beach say to the ocean after the tide came back in?

"Long time, no sea."

What is a maths teacher's favourite season?

Sum-mer.

What is a witch's favourite class in school?

*Spell*ing.

Why should you never use a broken pencil?

Because it's pointless!

What letter contains the most water?

The "C."

What did the toilet do when it got embarrassed?

It flushed.

What is a snowman's favourite cereal?

Frosties.

Why did the teacher put on his sunglasses in the classroom?

Because his students were so bright!

How do you wrap up an umbrella?

With a rainbow!

Where do vampires keep their money?

At the blood bank.

What are you when you find money in the dirt?

Filthy rich!

What did the snowman say when he left the store?

"Have an *ice* day."

Why was the computer in the hospital?

Because it had a virus!

What's got four wheels and flies?

A smelly car.

What do you call a snowman's kids?

*Chill*dren.

DID YOU KNOW...?
A person's sneeze can travel at speeds up to 100 miles per hour.

What do they use on building sites at the North Pole?

Crane-deer.

What did the snowman do when he was mad at his girlfriend?

He gave her the cold shoulder.

What does a snowman use for transport when his car is in the garage?

His icycle.

What did Cinderella lose after going scuba diving?

Her glass *flipper*.

Why do celebrities stay cool all the time?

Because they have so many fans.

What would you get if you cross a zombie and a snowman?

Frostbite.

What time is it when you can see a full moon right above your bed?

Time to fix the whole in your roof!

What did the ball of string dress up as for Halloween?

Frankentwine.

How do mountains stay warm in the winter?

By wearing ice caps.

TIME FOR A TONGUE TWISTER...
If two witches were watching two watches, which witch would watch which watch?

What happened when the snowman was hit by the snowball?

He was knocked out cold.

Where did the astronaut go when she got married?

On her honey*moon*.

Where do city pigs live?

In *sty*scrapers

What do you call someone who casts spells at the beach?

A sand*witch*.

Why does Dracula like maths?

Because he loves to *count*.

What do you call it when a snowman has a tantrum?

A meltdown.

How do you farm icicles?

Use a snow plow.

Why did the boy go out in the snow?

Because he wanted to be cool.

Who is the snowman's uncle married to?

Aunt Arctica.

Who do ghosts go on dates with?

Their *ghoul*friends.

What did the ice on the road say to the car?

"Wanna go for a spin?"

What do farmers use to mend holes in their trousers?

Cabbage patches.

How do snow globes feel when they're scared?

A little shaken.

What musical note has the best vision?

C sharp.

Why can't your hand be 12 inches in length?

Because then it would be a *foot*.

Why did the painting get arrested?

Because it had been *framed*.

DID YOU KNOW...?
Australia is wider than the moon.

Why are 3, 7, and 21 so strange?
Because they're odd.

Why was the sailor so cold?
Because his boat was in the har*brrr*.

What do stars put their drinks in?
*Sun*glasses.

What's a pirate's favourite exercise?
The plank.

Why did the maths teacher wear a plaster cast on his leg?
Because he broke his *angle*.

Why did the man buy a brand new lamp?
To see things in a new light.

Where do pirates buy their hooks?

At second hand shops.

When is the best time to buy a boat?

When it's on *sail*.

What do you call the wife of a hippy?

Mississippi.

What do you call someone who makes wooden vehicles?

A *car*penter.

Sally has 100 doughnuts. She eats 75 of them. What does she have now?

A stomach ache.

What's invisible and smells like bananas?

A monkey's burps!

What did the pirate say when chopping down a tree in winter?

"Shiver me timberrrrrrr!"

Where do you buy replacement clock parts?

At the *second hand* shop.

Why was the right angle so hot?

Because it was 90 degrees.

What is the circumference of a Halloween lamp divided by the diameter?

Pumpkin *Pi*.

Why did four and eight not want to fight 33, 41, and 7?

Because the *odds* were against them!

Why should you never flush wooden shoes down the toilet?

Because they will *clog* it!

What do you call an emotional horse?

Unstable.

What do you call a fake phone?

A Phony.

What did the priest say before getting rid of the mosquitos?

Let us *spray*.

What happened when the man tried to catch the steam?

He *mist.*

Why is a computer like a window?

They both have screens.

Why was the calendar afraid it was going to die?

Because its days were numbered.

Why was 6 afraid of 7?

Because 7 8 9.

What do you call a boomerang that won't come back?

A stick.

Why was the sand wet?

Because the seaweed.

What is green and not heavy?

Light green.

What do you call a bad hairdo?

A hair "don't."

Why are trampolines scary?

They make you jump.

What do ghosts have for pudding?

I scream.

What wobbles when it flies?

A jelly copter.

Why was the broom late for school?

He over swept.

Where do pencils go on holiday?

Pencil-vania.

What's orange and sounds like a parrot?

A carrot.

What's white and goes upwards?

A confused snowflake.

DID YOU KNOW...?

Human ears never stop growing.

How did the barber win the race?

He knew a short cut.

Where does the General keep his armies?

Up his sleevies.

How do we know that the ocean is friendly?

It waves.

What did the right eye say to the left eye?

Between you and me something smells.

What's a skeleton's favourite musical instrument?

A trombone.

What did the policeman say to his tummy?

Freeze, you're under a vest!

Why didn't the skeleton go to ball?

It had nobody to go with.

What did the shy traffic lights say to the car?

Look away, I'm changing.

When has the moon had too much to eat?

When it's full.

What did the mummy star call the baby star?

Sun.

What game do you play at the barber?

Musical *hairs*.

What did the paper say when it ripped?

"This is *tear*ibble."

What do clouds wear in their hair?

Rain*bows*.

What musical instrument do you keep in your bathroom?

A tube-a toothpaste.

Cars run on diesel, what do people run on?

The ground.

What kind of nail should you not hit with a hammer?

Your fingernail!

What did the zombie call its mother?

Mummy.

What did the zombie call its father?

Deady.

What happens when snowmen go to heaven?

The become snow angels.

What did the man's nose say to the man's finger?

"Don't pick on me!"

Where do young cars go to play?

To the car *park*.

What did the pilot say when he met another pilot?

"High!"

What do you call a watering can that doesn't work?

A watering *can*'t.

What is the king of the school bag?

The ruler.

What did the brush do when it was tired?

It fell a*sweep*.

What do you call a crazy balloon?

A Bal*loony*.

What do you call an adult balloon?

A Blown-up.

How do scientists keep their breaths fresh?

With experi*mints*.

What did the pirate say when he turned 80 years old?

Aye matey.

What is a doctor's favourite part of the body?

The *heal*.

Which planet is the most musical?

Nep*tune*.

Why did the girl put sugar on her pillow?

Because she wanted sweet dreams.

Why do pirates have so much paint?

Because they love *arrr*t.

What do rainclouds wear under their clothes?

*Thunder*wear.

What do snowmen say when they don't know the answer?

"I have *snow* idea."

What do you get when you cross a musical instrument with a dog?

A trum*pet*.

Why did the teddy bear not eat anymore?

Because it was *stuffed*.

What did the reading teacher take when he went fishing?

Bookworms!

Which kind of tree can you hold in your hand?

A palm!

DID YOU KNOW...?
The first home video game invented was in 1967.

Why did the man use scissors to get home quicker?

Because he wanted to take a short cut.

What time is it when your clock says 2500?

Time to get a new clock!

How do you fix a Halloween lantern?

With a pumpkin patch.

Why can you always trust dentists?

Because they always tell the *tooth* the whole tooth and nothing but the tooth.

What would you call a funny mountain?

*Hilll*arious.

What kind of music do balloons hate?

Pop music.

What do monsters use after they've washed their hair?

Scare conditioner.

What do you sweep the floor with when it's cold?

A *brrr*ush.

What goes "Ha ha ha.....THUD!"?

Someone laughing their head off.

How did the man make the skeleton laugh?

He tickled its funny bone.

What kind of vehicle do you drive with your foot?

A toe truck.

What do snowmen sleep under?

Sheets of ice and blankets of snow!

Why did the toilet paper roll down the hill?

To get to the bottom.

What do you call a man in a big paper bag?

Russell

What do you get when you cross a snowman with a vampire

Frostbite!

What do you call a man with gravy on his head?

Stew

What do you call a woman with a pet tortoise?

Shelley

What do you call a woman who likes doing laundry?

Peggy

What do you call a woman who can jump across a river?

Bridget

What do you call a woman who likes windy weather?

Gail

What do you call a man floating in a swimming pool?

Bob

WHaT DO YOu cAll a MAn wHO lOVes eXerCIsiNg?

JiM

What do you call a man who keeps rabbits in his trousers?

Warren

What's grey and goes round and round?

An elephant in a washing machine!

What do you call a man who can stop water?

Adam

What do you call a man who can't stand up?

Neal

What do you call a man lying on your doorstep?

Matt

What do you call a man with a seagull on his head?

Cliff

What do you call a man who's good at digging holes?

Doug

What do you call a man who is not so good at digging holes?

Douglas (Dug less)

What do you call a woman with a frog on her head?

Lilly

What do you call a man with a toilet on his head?

Lou

What is red and smells like blue paint?

Red paint.

What did the policeman say when he was called to a robbery at the aquarium?

There's something fishy going on here.

What happens to two angels marry each other?

They live harpily ever after.

If you throw a white stone into the Black Sea, what will it become?

Wet.

Sport

Why is Cinderella no good at football?

She keeps running away from the ball.

How do footballers stay cool?

They sit down next to their fans.

Why don't fish play tennis?

They're scared of the net.

Why did the golfer put on a new sock?

Because he got a *hole in one.*

What do you call a pig that's an expert in karate?

A pork chop.

What do you call a group of golf balls?

A golf *club.*

What do you call a girl standing in the middle of a tennis court?

Annette.

Which athlete is the warmest in winter?

The long jumper.

When is a football pitch like a triangle?

When someone takes a corner.

What is a ghost's favourite position?

Ghoulkeeper.

Why are footballers like babies?

They both dribble.

Which football team loves ice-cream?

Aston Vanilla.

What did the manager do when the pitch flooded?

Sent on the subs.

What do you get when you cross a champion boxer with a comedian?

A really good punchline.

Why was the millipede dropped from the rugby team?

He took too long to put his boots on.

What is green and can jump a mile in a minute?

A grasshopper with the hiccups.

What is a frog's favourite game?

Croack-et.

Why is a brilliant football player like a magician?

They both do hat-tricks.

Christmas Jokes

What song do elves sing to Santa?

"*Freeze* a Jolly Good Fellow."

What does Santa get when he crosses a skunk with a bell?

Jingle *smells*.

What do monkeys sing at Christmas?

Jungle bells.

What do rhinos hang on their Christmas trees?

*Horn*aments.

Why is it so cold around Christmas time?

Because it's Decem*brrr*.

What is red, white, and blue at Christmas?

A candy cane that is feeling sad.

What's it called when Santa's helper takes a picture of herself?

An *elf*ie.

What did Santa say when he stepped in a puddle?

It must have *rained-here.*

Why is there one less letter in the alphabet at Christmas?

Because there's No*el.*

What does Santa wear when he goes down the Chimney?

His soot.

Who says, "Oh, oh, oh"?

Father Christmas going backwards!

What is Santa's favourite garden tool?

A ho-ho-ho.

What do you call a dog on the beach at Christmas time?

Sandy paws.

What do Santa's helpers learn when they go to school?

The *elf*abet.

What does Santa use to help him walk?

A candy cane.

Dinosaur Jokes

What do you get when dinosaurs crash their cars?

Tyrannosaurus wrecks.

What do you call a one-eyed dinosaur?

A Doyathinkhesawus.

What do you call a T-Rex when it's asleep?

A dino-snore.

What do you call a T-Rex that talks and talks and talks?

A dino-bore.

What do you call a T-Rex that's been beaten in a fight?

Dino-sore.

What do you call a frightened dinosaur?

Nervous Rex.

What should you do if you find a dinosaur in your bed?

Find somewhere else to sleep.

Which dinosaurs make the best policemen?

Tricera-cops.

What does a triceratops sit on?

Its tricera-bottom.

DID YOU KNOW...?

The Stegosaurus dinosaur was over 9 metres long but its brain was only the size of a walnut.

What do you get when you cross a dinosaur with fireworks?

Dinomite.

Why can't you hear a pterosaur using the toilet?

It has a silent "p."

Which dinosaur could jump higher than a house?

All of them - houses can't jump.

Why didn't the dinosaur cross the road?

There were no roads when they existed.

What kind of dinosaur loves to sleep?

A stega-snore-us.

Romantic Jokes

What do you call a small valentine card?
Valen*tiny card.*

What did the volcano say to her boyfriend?
"I *lava* you!"

What did the pig get on Valentine's Day?
A hog and a kiss!

Why did the woman's husband go to jail?
Because he stole her heart.

Why did the triangle get so many love letters?
Because he was acute triangle.

TIME FOR A TONGUE TWISTER...
A tricky, frisky snake with sixty super scaly stripes.

What do you get a sailor on Valentine's Day?

Forget-me-*knots*.

What is a pig's favourite romantic holiday?

Valen*swine*'s day.

What did the bird call his girlfriend?

*Tweet*heart.

What is the best fruit to eat on Valentine's Day?

Dates.

What kind of vegetables do you get on Valentine's Day?

Cauli*flowers*.

What did the bell give his girlfriend?

A ring.

When does the sun give love letters?

On Valen*shine's* Day.

What should you give a carpet that you love?

Rugs and kisses.

What did the painter call her boyfriend?

Her sweet*art*.

What did the mitten say to his wife?

"I glove you."

What did one shoe say to the other shoe on Valentine's day?

"You're *boot*iful."

Doctor, Doctor Jokes

Doctor, doctor, I can't breathe!
Are you choking?
No, I'm being serious!

Doctor, doctor, I really want to get on a skateboard.
I wouldn't do that, you'll probably go downhill fast.

Doctor, doctor, I'm think I'm having memory loss?
When did this start?
When did what start?

DID YOU KNOW...?
If you walked for 12 hours a day, it would take 690 days to walk right around the world.

Doctor, doctor, I feel like I've turned into a goat!
How long have you been feeling this way?
Ever since I was a kid.

Doctor, doctor, I feel like I've turned into a dog!
How long have you been feeling this way?
Ever since I was a puppy.

Doctor, doctor, I'm worried I've turned invisible.
Who said that?

Doctor, doctor, I really do feel like I'm a dog.
Alright, have a seat on the couch and I'll take a look at you
I'm not allowed on the couch!

Doctor, doctor, you've got to help me out...
Sure, the exit's over there!

Doctor, doctor, I have a boiling fever!
Alright, just simmer down.

Doctor, doctor, I think I only have 60 seconds to live!
I'll be with you in a minute.

Doctor, doctor...
You need new glasses?
How did you know?
Because you're talking to my plant.

Doctor, doctor, everyone says I'm a huge liar!
I don't believe you.

DID YOU KNOW...?
Frogs drink water through their skin.

Doctor, doctor, I feel like a caterpillar!
Oh, don't worry, you'll change soon!

Doctor, doctor, it hurts when I press my finger here... and here... and here. In fact it hurts wherever I press my finger, what's wrong with me?
You have a broken finger.

Doctor, doctor, I've got a really bad cold.
Try some orange juice it will help kill the germs.
OK but how do I get the germs to drink the orange juice...?

Doctor, doctor, I need something to stop me from seeing double.
Here, take this pill.
Which one?

Doctor, doctor, I feel like I'm a pack of cards.
I'll deal with you later!

Doctor, doctor, it seems like I'm being ignored by everyone!
Next please!

Doctor, doctor, I need something for my hair that's been falling out.
You could try putting it in a plastic bag.

Doctor, doctor, an alligator bit off my left arm and left leg.
Don't worry, you'll be all right.

Doctor, doctor, I'm worried I've turned into some curtains!
Pull yourself together.

Doctor, doctor, I keep finding custard in one ear, and jelly in the other.
Hmm it seems you are a trifle deaf.

Doctor, doctor, I keep seeing an insect flying about wherever I go.
Don't worry, that's just a bug that's going around.

TIME FOR A TONGUE TWISTER...

Eleven elves licked eleven little liquorice lollipops.

Riddles

Q: What has hands, but no fingers?

A: A clock.

Q: A pirate sailed to an island on Wednesday. He stayed there for three days and sailed away from the island on Thursday. How is that possible?

A: The name of his ship was Wednesday.

Q: What is blue at first but is red when you're finished?

A: A blue book. When you're finished, it's been *read*.

Q: Tim shaved twelve times in one day. At the end of the day, however, he had a full beard. How?

A: Tim was a barber.

Q: I sit when I stand and I jump when I walk. What am I?

A: A Kangaroo.

Q: You can hold it without using your hands or your arms. What is it?

A: Your breath.

Q: What roars and has an eye but cannot see or walk?

A: A hurricane.

Q: What three letters can turn a boy into a man?

A: Age.

Q: What is always going up but can never go down?

A: Your age.

Q: What can be served, but never eaten?

A: A volleyball!

Q: This is lighter than air, yet you cannot hold if for more than five minutes. What is it?

A: Your breath.

Q: It's tall when it's young and short when it's old. What is it?

A: A candle.

Q: If you feed this, it gets bigger. If you give it water you will kill it. What is it?

A: Fire.

Q: If you walk in a room with a match, a candle, a fireplace, and a stove, which should you light first?

A: The match!

DID YOU KNOW...?

No piece of square paper can be folded in half more than 7 times.

Q: What should you never buy with "no strings attached?"

A: A kite.

Q: What can travel all over the world but stay in the corner the entire time?

A: A stamp.

Q: What comes once in a second, twice in a week, but never in a month?

A: The letter "E."

Q: Tell me how many letters are in the alphabet.

A: There are 11. T-H-E-A-L-P-H-A-B-E-T.

Q: Janet and Tim were married. Janet passed Tim on the street but didn't say anything to him, even though she saw him. In fact, she had never met him before. How is this possible?

A: Janet and Tim were married, just not to each other.

Q: What do cats have that no other animal does?

A: Kittens!

Q: If you share this, you will not have it anymore. What is it?

A: A secret.

DID YOU KNOW...?

A pet hamster can run up to 8 miles a night on a wheel.

Q: Megan was driving a racing car and passed the person in second place. What place is Megan in now?

A: Second place.

Q: What starts with "M," ends in "X," and contains dozens of letters?

A: Mailbox.

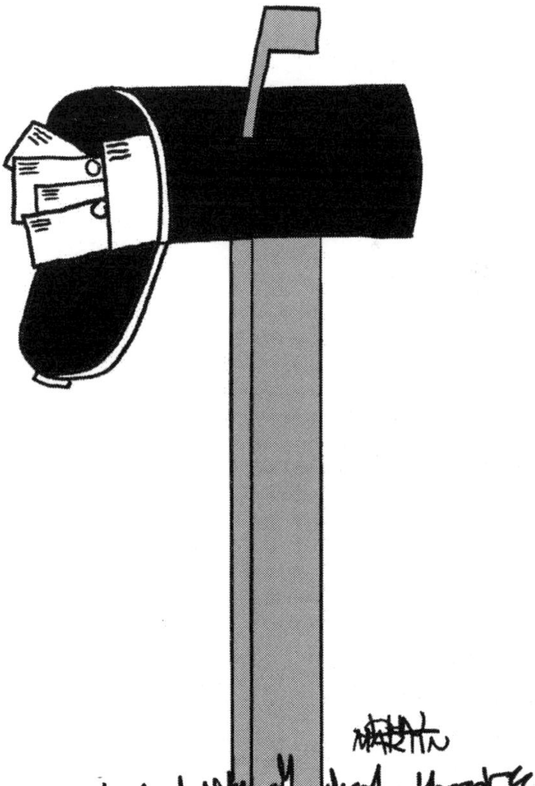

Q: What will you find at the end of the rainbow?

A: The letter "w."

Q: It won't cry if you skin it, but you probably will. What is it?

A: An onion.

Q: This is full of holes yet can still hold plenty of water. What is it?

A: A sponge.

Q: A man was in a rowing boat when it capsized. He fell into the water, and his clothes were soaking wet. However, not a single hair on his head was. How is that possible?

A: The man was bald.

Q: There are five doughnuts on the table. If you take away two, how many doughnuts do you have?

A: Two doughnuts. If you take away two, YOU have two.

Q: What sounds just like you but is not you?

A: Your echo.

TIME FOR A TONGUE TWISTER...
I can think of six thin things, but I can think of six thick things too.

Q: If you take away two from this odd number it becomes even. What is it?

A: Eleven. Take away the "E" and the "L" at the beginning and it becomes "even."

Q: What can be made and broken, but cannot be fixed?

A: A rule.

Q: What has branches but no trunk or leaves?

A: A bank.

Q: What falls on a cold day without getting hurt?

A: Snow.

Q: You get this every single birthday. What is it?

A: Older!

Q: Mr. Morris's restaurant was busy all day, even though there wasn't a single person who ate there. How is that possible?

A: All the people that ate there were married.

Q: If you say its name, it disappears. What is it?

A: Silence.

Q: How can a man, a woman, and their seven children all be underneath one umbrella without getting wet?

A: If it's not raining.

Q: Freddy was seven on his last birthday and will be nine on his next birthday. How is this possible?

A: Today is his eighth birthday.

DID YOU KNOW...?

About 70% of an adult's body is water and water covers around 70% of the earth

Q: You can catch this, but you cannot throw it. What is it?

A: A cold.

Q: A girl was standing on a ladder and fell off. However, she did not get hurt. How is this possible?

A: She was standing on the bottom rung.

Q: What has a mouth but cannot talk, and a bed but cannot sleep?

A: A river.

TIME FOR A TONGUE TWISTER...

This one is thought to be the hardest tongue twister in the English language!

The sixth sick sheik's sixth sheep's sick

Printed in Great Britain
by Amazon

62731122R00099